CONTENTS

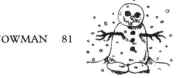

"There's a monster under my bed,"
Emma told Dad.

EMMA'S MONSTER

Seven warm and imaginative read-aloud stories about a small girl and her friendly monster.

Marjorie Darke has written many books for children. Two of her novels for older readers, *A Question of Courage* and *The First of Midnight*, were shortlisted for the Guardian Fiction Award – and both have been dramatized and broadcast on radio. Several of her stories for younger children have been read on television. She is the author of another read-aloud story collection, *Just Bear and Friends*.

Monster went splat *in the paint tin,*
sending up a shower of brown spots.

Emma's Monster

Written by
MARJORIE DARKE

Illustrated by
SHELAGH MCNICHOLAS

WALKER BOOKS
AND SUBSIDIARIES

LONDON • BOSTON • SYDNEY

For Helen and Alexander

The first two stories in this book were
originally commissioned by Ragdoll Productions
for "Pob's Programme" (Channel 4)

First published 1992 by
Walker Books Ltd, 87 Vauxhall Walk
London SE11 5HJ

This edition published 1999

2 4 6 8 10 9 7 5 3 1

Text © 1992 Marjorie Darke
Illustrations © 1992 Shelagh MᶜNicholas
Cover illustration © 1999 Paul Howard

This book has been typeset in Plantin.

Printed in England by Clays Ltd, St Ives plc

British Library Cataloguing in Publication Data
A catalogue record for this book is
available from the British Library.

ISBN 0-7445-7229-0

EMMA'S MONSTER

"I don't want to go to bed," Emma said.

"It's half past six. You always go to bed now," said Dad.

"But I don't want to," Emma said, very loud.

Dad looked at her. "Why not?"

"Because there's a monster under my bed," Emma told him.

Dad put down his book. "I hoovered under your bed today. I didn't find any monster."

"He lives in a hole," Emma explained. "He only comes out at night."

Dad stood up. "Tell you what. How if I come upstairs with you and we look together? If the monster is there I'll pick him up and take him away."

"He'll bite you." Emma showed all her teeth. "He growls URRRG, and his teeth *snap snap*, and he's got big red eyes."

Dad laughed. "I want to meet this splendid monster of yours. Come on!" and he went with Emma up to her room.

They kneeled down and looked under the bed. There was a slipper, a ball, and a feather. But no monster.

"He's hiding in that hole." Emma pointed behind her bed.

A mouse-sized hole!

"He must be a very little monster to squeeze in there," Dad said.

"Sometimes he's little. Sometimes he grows as big as a bus," Emma said.

Dad looked surprised. "A bus? In here? He wouldn't fit."

"He'll bite you."
Emma showed all her teeth.

"A small bus." Emma took off her jumper.

Dad helped with shoelaces, and when she was in her pyjamas and had cleaned her teeth, tucked her up in bed. "When you see the monster, tell him to come and watch telly with me."

"He doesn't like telly." Emma wriggled down under the bedclothes.

Dad kissed her. "Ask him and see. You never know!" And he went out, leaving the door ajar.

Emma lay in bed. The moon came in and made silver stripes on her wall. A moth flew round and round. She was almost asleep when…

"URRRG!"

The monster's noise! Her eyelids flew open.

"URRRG! URRRRRRG!"

She was very surprised and just a bit

Emma wriggled down under the bedclothes.

scared. No pretending, this monster was real! She opened her mouth to shout for Dad.

"*Snuffle-snuffle! Chatter-chatter! Rattle! Hiccup!*"

It didn't sound like a fierce monster.

Emma shut her mouth and wriggled to the edge of her bed. Carefully she looked over and under.

Two big red upside-down eyes stared back.

A very small monster. Not fierce at all. He was shivering. His long arms shook, his wild wild hair trembled, his big teeth chattered, his pointed ears quivered and his little round face looked crinkled with cold.

Cold and *scared*, Emma thought, feeling not scared at all. She got out of bed and picked up her jumper. "Put this on and get warm."

The monster crept from under the bed and Emma helped him put on the jumper. The arms were rather short, but he didn't mind.

Then they played ball. And blowing the feather. The monster's long arms reached the other side of the room to catch the ball, to pick up the feather. He grew, not as big as a bus, but chair-sized – and shrank again. His big red eyes shone bright as torches, so he and Emma sat in bed and looked at a picture book until they were tired. Then they lay down and went to sleep together.

"Your monster didn't turn up after all," Dad said to Emma at breakfast next morning.

"Yes he did," Emma said. "But he didn't want to come downstairs. I like telly but he doesn't. I *told* you."

*Emma thought about it
while she cut paper shapes.*

TOOTHACHE

"We'll go to the dentist tomorrow," Dad said.

"Why?" asked Emma. She was cutting paper shapes.

"So he can look at our teeth."

"I'll go another day," Emma said. "I'm busy tomorrow."

Dad started to wash up. "The dentist is busy every day. He's made a special time to see us tomorrow. It wouldn't be friendly if we didn't turn up. Think about it."

Emma thought about it while she cut paper shapes. Then forgot about it while she rode her trike, played ball, went to the shops with Dad, ate her tea, put on her pyjamas, had a bedtime story.

After the story she went upstairs to bed.

"Don't forget to clean your teeth," Dad called.

But she did forget, because on the way she stopped to say good night to a spider who lived on the top stair. He had lived there a long time, but tonight he had gone.

"He's gone to see his gran," Emma said. "Then he had an ice-cream. Then he felt sick. Then he went to hospital." She went into her room. "Then the nurse put him to bed." She climbed into her bed. "Then he had ... some ... medicine..." Then she went to sleep.

In the middle of the night something woke her up. For a minute she thought of going to find Dad, when...

"URRRRRRRRRRG!" the something said. "OWOWOWOWOWEEEEEEK!"

In the middle of the night
something woke Emma up.

Emma smiled. She hung over the side of her bed.

Underneath, two big shiny red eyes looked back at her. Tears spouted down two little crinkly cheeks, dripped off a wobbly chin and fell on two furry feet.

Her friend the monster who lived under the bed!

"Whatever's the matter?" Emma asked.

The monster opened his wide mouth and she saw two rows of very green teeth.

"You've got toothache!" she said. "What did I tell you about remembering to clean your teeth?"

The monster hung his head.

"Come out!"

He came out, moaning and groaning. His wild wild hair was all limp and damp. Even his knees were wet. Emma felt very sorry for him. She fetched a warm scarf to tie round his aching head, climbed back into bed and cuddled him until they both went to sleep.

"Don't forget we're going to the dentist today," Dad said next morning.

"Monster can go instead of me," Emma said. "He's got toothache."

"Poor old thing!" Dad said. "Why don't we all go? You can tell the dentist about your monster's toothache, and show your monster the ceiling game."

Emma liked the ceiling game. You lay in the dentist's chair and walked your eyes along a road pinned to the ceiling. Past the Sweet Mountain, through Toothache Gate to the Red Apple Orchard, and on to the Toothbrush Forest.

"All right," she said.

But when she went to fetch him, Monster played one of his tricks. He shrank as small as a flea and hopped into Emma's pocket. He wouldn't come out, even in the dentist's room. But he made noises.

"URRRRRRG ... OWOWOWOWOWEEEEEEK!"

The dentist was surprised.

"It's Monster," Emma explained. "He's got toothache."

"I've got the very thing for that." The dentist pulled open a drawer. "Pink Monster Toothpaste! Hold the tube while I look at your teeth. I'll fix your monster afterwards."

So Emma held the Pink Monster Toothpaste tube, and her eyes walked along the ceiling road. By the time she reached Toothbrush Forest, the dentist had finished.

But Monster still hid in her pocket.

"Never mind," said the dentist. "Make him clean his teeth. That will send his toothache away."

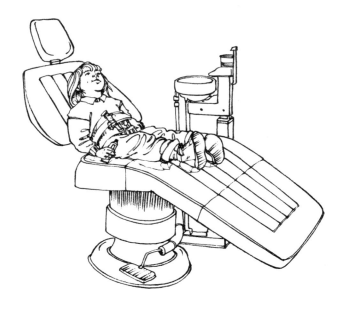

Emma took Monster back home and showed him how to clean his teeth properly. Bottom up. Top down. And all round the back.

Then they ran races until it was time for cheese on toast, with a red apple for afters.

*"What's it like at playschool?" Emma asked
Dad as he helped put on her shoes.*

PLAYSCHOOL DAY

Emma was going to playschool. She had been waiting to go for one, two, three weeks. Now here was the very first playschool day.

"What's it like at playschool?" Emma asked Dad as he helped put on her shoes.

"Fun," Dad said. "There's sand to dig in, and you can paint pictures, and go on the climbing frame, and sing songs, and there are lots of other children doing all these things with you. But we've talked about this before."

"I know." Emma wriggled her toes. "I just wanted to hear again."

Dad tied her laces.

23

"I don't think my monster is well enough to go to playschool today," Emma said.

"Your monster?" Dad asked as if he didn't know.

"He lives in that hole in the wall under my bed, remember?" Emma reminded him.

"Oh yes ... of course." Dad fetched her anorak.

"He sneezed and sneezed last night. *Atishoooooo* ... like that. He told me his throat was sore."

"In that case he'd better stay at home until he gets better." Dad held out the anorak. "Put your arms in."

Emma put one arm in. Then took it out. "I'd better stay too. In case he gets lonely. I'll go to playschool another day."

Dad thought for a moment. "If I were your monster, I'd want you to go to playschool. Then you could tell me all about it when you got home again."

Emma shook her head. "He wants to go *with* me. The very first day. She untied her laces and kicked off her shoes. "If I go by myself he'll be cross. He'll growl ... GRRRRR. And bite with his big teeth ... like that!" She snapped her teeth. "He'll bite you, and me ... he'll bite *everybody*."

"I see," said Dad. "We can't have that!" Picking up his newspaper, he sat down to read.

Emma watched him for a bit. Then she watched a fly crawl up the window and down again. Outside the sun had come out and somebody began to play a jingly tune. She knew that tune and who was playing it.

"Dad," she said. "Monster's sore throat might get better if he had an ice-cream. Then we could both go to playschool."

Dad looked at her over the top of his

Emma crept under the bed and peered down the hole in the wall.

newspaper. "Is that so? But Monster isn't here. The ice-cream would melt and drip on the floor with nobody to lick it."

"I'll fetch him while you fetch the ice-cream," Emma said, and ran upstairs.

But when she looked under the bed there was nothing but dust.

She crept under the bed and peered down the hole in the wall. It was empty.

So she looked behind the door – only her dressing gown hanging on a hook.

She hunted in the bathroom and the airing cupboard. Nothing but soap in the bath and towels in the cupboard.

Emma went slowly back downstairs.

No Dad.

But two big watery red eyes stared at her from a little crinkly face. Monster – sitting in Dad's chair! He smiled, showing his big green teeth, wrinkled his flat nose and sneezed: "*Atishoooooo!*" like that – just as Dad came back holding an ice-cream cornet.

"Are you catching a cold?" Dad asked.

"Not me. That was Monster," Emma said. "And you should have brought *two* ice-creams – one for me and one for him."

Dad looked around. "Is he here? I can't see him."

But Emma could. Monster had played a trick, shrunk very small and jumped to sit on the edge of the cornet. He was licking ice-cream with his long yellow tongue.

While they shared the ice-cream, Emma told him all about playschool.

"You can dig in the sand and paint pictures and climb and sing and have fun with the children. Shall we go together?"

Monster nodded his head so hard his wild wild hair flew out like a mop.

Emma ate the last cornet crumb. "We're ready to go to playschool now," she told Dad.

"Are you really sure?" he asked.

"Really, really, really!"

Emma began to put on her shoes.

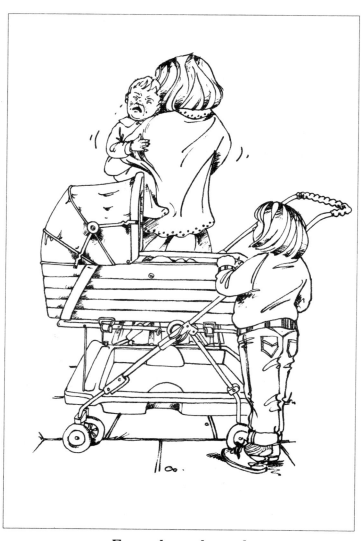

*Emma hopped round
the other side for a better look.*

GEORGE

There was a loud knock on the door and an even louder: "WAAAAAAH!"

"I'll go!" Emma shouted up the stairs to Dad. He was getting ready for his training run.

Emma was getting ready as well. Half a foot was stuck into one of her trainers but wouldn't go any further. The lace was in a knot. She had to hop to reach the door.

"Hello, Emma!" said George's mum, lifting George from his pram.

"WAAAAAAAAAH!" bawled George, and flopped over her shoulder.

Emma hopped round the other side for a better look. His face looked like a radish.

Red and bulgy. His mouth was open, getting ready for another: "WWWAAAAAAAAHHH!"

"He's cross," Emma said.

George showed her just how cross: "WWAAAAHWAAAAHWWAAHIC!"

His mum shook her head. "He's been like this half the night. New tooth coming, I shouldn't wonder."

Emma nodded. She knew all about toothache. "I made Monster clean his teeth when they ached. Then they got better." She peered into George's pink mouth. "He hasn't got any to clean."

"Not yet." George's mum brought George into the house. "And who is this monster?"

"My friend," Emma explained. "He lives under my bed and... Oh! Look!" She pointed at the door under the stairs which had opened just a crack. Two big red eyes shone from the darkness.

"What is it?" George's mum was looking through into the kitchen.

"Not there … *there*! It's Monster." But Monster had vanished.

"Oh, I see," George's mum said in the sort of voice that meant she didn't.

Emma rushed to the cupboard under the stairs, meaning to drag out Monster so George's mum really would see. She tugged so hard the door banged against the stairs.

George howled.

"What a din!" Dad said, coming downstairs. "Emma, what are you doing?"

Emma didn't answer. Inside the cupboard, brooms and umbrellas clattered about. The dustpan fell on the Hoover. A pile of paint cans toppled over. A box of old Christmas cards and bits of tinsel went flying. Emma was shouting, "Come out!" Her voice sounded like a bee in a bucket.

*"Wait!" Emma squeaked,
and tried to wriggle free.*

"I know you're there. Come out!"

"I think it's you who should come out!" Dad leaned in and grabbed her.

"Wait!" she squeaked, and tried to wriggle free. Monster's wild wild hair was sticking up from behind a cardboard box.

But Dad didn't wait. He hauled her out and dumped her on the mat at the foot of the stairs.

Emma was very cross. "I said wait. Now you've frightened him."

"Who?"

"Monster, of course. He'll hide again. He might even run away and never come back..." She stopped as Monster popped his head out of the cupboard. His pointed ears curled tight, then uncurled. All his green teeth, top and bottom, showed in a big grin. With a quick flick of his long yellow tongue he licked the tip of his nose, and winked. Emma had to laugh.

"That's better," Dad said, with his back to Monster. "I want that cupboard tidy before I get home."

"I'll do it as soon as I come back," Emma promised.

"And where are you off to?"

"We're training together. I told you."

Dad sighed.

George howled.

Emma tried to pull on her trainers to show she meant what she said ... and broke the lace.

George's mum said quickly, "How about helping to push the pram into the garden, Emma? George needs a nap. Then you and I can play a game together. What do you say?"

"No!" Emma kicked off her trainer and sat down on the stairs.

Dad squatted by her and put his hands on her shoulders. "Emma, we've talked about this. If you came with me you'd get left behind. You can't run as fast as I do."

"You can run as slow as I do." Emma blinked hard.

"I promise we'll both run slow tomorrow." Dad stood up.

Emma was just going to hang on to his legs so he couldn't run fast *or* slow, when she caught sight of Monster again. Small Monster this time – doing cartwheels along the top of the door. Emma watched to see if he fell off. By the time he had safely reached the end, George was back in his pram and Dad had gone.

"It's your fault," Emma said to the top of the door. "You just wait!" But Monster had already slithered down and disappeared.

"Help me park this noisy boy in the

George shouted all the way to the apple tree.

garden," said George's mum. "Then what about a water game in the sink?"

Emma opened her mouth to say "No", but decided on "Yes" instead. She liked water games.

George shouted all the way to the apple tree.

His mum put on the pram brake. "We'll leave him on his own for a bit. If we don't show our faces he'll soon drop asleep. He needs a nap."

They sneaked back to the house. On the way to the kitchen Emma looked into the cupboard under the stairs. "Don't show your face!" she called, in case Monster was listening. "George is having a nap."

But George didn't drop asleep. He yelled while Emma was putting on her plastic apron. He bawled all the time the tap was running. He roared as she pushed a bottle in the water and watched the rush of bubbles. As she poured water through a sieve, she could still hear him moaning and squeaking. But as she was stirring a whirlpool with a wooden spoon, George made a very different sort of noise. He made it twice. Three times.

Emma got off the stool. "I'm going to get my watering-can," she told George's mum, who was making a cup of tea. Opening the back door, she slipped into the garden.

The pram was jigging up and down. George's bare feet waved in the air. That was all right. But something else wasn't right – Monster, dancing along the pram handle.

"Hey!" Emma bounded across the grass. "I told you not to show your face."

Monster didn't listen. He leapt on to the pram hood. Hung upside down. Stretched

The pram was jigging up and down.
George's bare feet waved in the air.

out his wide mouth with his skinny fingers. Screwed up his eyes. Stuck out his long yellow tongue.

George chuckled, grabbed ... and Monster let himself be caught.

George tried to eat him, but Monster sprang into the air, turned a couple of somersaults and nose-dived down the side of the pram mattress.

"Hey!" George's mum was hurrying across the grass. She sounded cross. "Emma, I thought I told you..." She stopped, gazing into the pram.

George beamed, showing his pink gums. His fists waved.

George's mum was beaming now. "Why, look, Emma!"

Emma looked, but she couldn't see Monster anywhere.

"Look how he's smiling. You've cheered

him up!" George's mum gave her a squeeze.

"It was Monster, not me," Emma said.

But George's mum didn't seem to hear. She was too busy feeling the tiny new tooth.

The postman put his hands over his ears.
"I'm not that far away!"

NIPPERGYM

"IT'S NIPPERGYM DAY!" Emma yelled over the gate to the milkman.

He waved a bottle of milk at her.

"IT'S NIPPERGYM DAY!" she bellowed to the postman as he came through the gate. "CAN I TAKE THE LETTERS?"

The postman put his hands over his ears. "I'm not that far away!" He took two letters from his bag. "Give them to your dad, mind. And do a handstand for me at Nippergym."

Indoors, Dad was roaring about with the Hoover.

"NIPPERGYM!" Emma reminded him in a loud voice, to make sure he heard. "HURRY

UP!" Leaving the letters on the table, she dashed out to talk to Freda.

Freda was the goat who lived over the fence from Emma's garden. Not on George's side: the other side. She was nibbling the hedge.

"I'M GOING TO NIPPERGYM, FREDA!" Emma bawled, rushing round into Freda's garden to scratch under her hairy chin. "There's a trampoline to jump on and a ladder to climb up and a wobbly beam and a tunnel and streamers and sticks and balls and beanbags. Afterwards George's mum gives me biscuits and squash."

Freda tried nibbling Emma's T-shirt.

"You can't eat *that*!" Emma pulled away and tore back into her own garden.

"NIPPERGYM!" she shouted over the fence to George's mum, who had her mouth full of pegs. George's dad was there too, weeding a flower-bed. He waved a dandelion at her.

Freda tried nibbling Emma's T-shirt.

George's mum had to hang up some more socks before she could speak. "George is coming with us today, Emma. He'll soon be big enough to join in. This is a first visit, so he can get used to it."

Emma bounced up and down, looking over the fence. "IT'S MONSTER'S FIRST DAY TOO!" She ran back into the house, dashing upstairs to tell him.

Monster was having one of his big-sized days. He was sitting in front of the mirror, wearing Emma's bobble cap and nothing else. He was pulling faces. Screwing up his squashy nose. Darting his long yellow tongue in and out, in and out. He had just started to puff his cheeks into balloons when he saw Emma watching. With a quick grab, he pulled the cap over his face and hid.

Emma whisked it off. "That's no good for Nippergym. You need gym stuff." She opened a drawer and scrabbled about. "Here!" she said, throwing shorts and a T-shirt at him. "Put those on. I'm taking you to Nippergym."

Monster's red eyes bulged. His green teeth began to chatter with fright.

"EERRK ... EEEEERRRK!" he squeaked. "GGGGRRRRFT ... JJJJGGGGGGRRFTTT!"

Emma frowned. "Don't be silly. Nippergym is fun." But before she could explain about the trampoline or the wobbly beam, he began to shrink...

Not fast this time. In stages.

Now he was the size of her teddy bear...

Now just right to walk into her dolls' house...

But he didn't. Instead he went on shrinking until he was as small as a marble.

The big clothes fell on top of him. When

Emma picked them up, Monster had vanished.

She started hunting round her bedroom. She poked in corners, peered under her bed, the chest of drawers, the wardrobe... All the time she was shouting, "DON'T BE A TWIT! COME OUT! GEORGE ISN'T SCARED. HE'S GOING TO NIPPERGYM. SO'S HENRY," slamming her door and tearing along towards Monster's favourite place – the warm airing cupboard. "SO'S ANISHA AND TIM AND KYLIE AND ERROL AND..."

"What's all the racket?" From the bottom of the staircase, Dad watched her through the bannisters.

"Emma, where are your trainers?" He came up three stairs. "And your tracksuit? You haven't even changed your jeans. Who was telling me to hurry up! Come on. We'll be late."

"What's all the racket?" Dad watched
Emma through the bannisters.

"It's all Monster's fault," Emma grumbled, scrambling out of her jeans and into her Nippergym clothes. She found a hairband to keep her fringe out of her eyes.

"He's scared. Isn't he silly?" she said to George in the car.

"I'm late because Monster was silly and hid and I tried to find him but I couldn't," she explained to Mrs Hopkins when she got to Nippergym.

"That's a new one!" Mrs Hopkins said. "Off with your tracksuit, Emma. Go and stand in the ring. Warm up first. Then it will be Jungle Day." She switched on the tape recorder. The music bounced and Emma bounced with it, landing next to Henry and his auntie who had come to help.

"I'm late because Monster was being a twit," she told them between bounces.

"A what?" Anisha asked, bouncing on her other side.

"A twit, a twit, a monster *twit!*" Emma chanted to the drum beat. "*Monster, monster, monster twit!*"

Everyone joined in: "*Monster, monster, monster, monster...*" until they were puffed and pink, and hot as any jungle.

Mrs Hopkins switched off the tape. "All right, choose what you want to be – monkeys, snakes, insects..."

"I'm a tiger!" Tim growled, and rushed at Kylie.

She bared her teeth. "I'm a *monster* tiger!"

Tim did a quick change; "I'm a monster monkey!" and scampered up the ladder-tree.

The room was suddenly full of monsters.

Errol flapped his arms. "I'm a monster parrot!"

Henry, with his auntie helping, bounced

on the trampoline. "Look at me, I'm a monster frog!"

Monster lions roared and roamed. Monster snakes slithered down the slide. Monster birds hopped and flapped. A monster caterpillar did forward rolls along the floor mattress.

Emma was being a monster ant. She crawled up the ladder, swung down again, shuffled along the wobbly beam, squeezed under the trestle bridge and into the tunnel, and found a monster worm.

"I wish Monster was here," Ant said to Worm. "He's missing all the fun. I *told* him."

Anisha Worm rolled over. "What monster?"

"*My* monster of course," Ant explained. "He lives under my bed. Sometimes he's as big as a bus and sometimes he makes himself small so he can hide in my pocket."

Worm sat up. "P'raps he's hiding now. P'raps he's going to jump out of your pocket – *jumpety bumpety crash* – like that," making the tunnel roll and shake as she fell out.

All of a sudden Monster *was* there, jumping and bumping up and down. Emma tried to grab him, but he bounded away. Scrambling after him, she found the room still full of the other monsters. They pounded about – feet stamping, elbows digging.

"MIND OUT!" Emma bellowed. "DON'T TREAD ON HIM!"

Everyone started shouting at once – "*Who...? What...? What is it...?*" – looking everywhere but where they were going. Pointing and shouting – "*There it is...! Where...? Under there... No, over here...*" –

as they fell over each other's feet, bumped into the tunnel, the ladder, the trestle bridge, while Monster scooted, hopped, dived under, scuttled out again, waving his arms and grinning.

"It's a mouse!" Henry's auntie climbed on a chair.

"A MONSTER MOUSE AND I'M A MONSTER CAT!" Henry yelled, tripping and shooting head first into the tunnel.

Emma was very glad when Mrs Hopkins clapped her hands and said it was parachute time. "Underneath, everyone!"

Mums and aunties made a space in the middle of the room. They spread the big

sheet and held it high. Emma knew what to do – stand, then kneel, then sit, then lie, while the parachute came gently floating down down down. Mostly she liked this, but today was different. Jungle monsters crowded under the parachute. But where was her Monster?

She saw George come crawling towards her, wanting to join in. He pushed between all the legs, right to the middle. Then he sat up, chuckling.

Emma was on her knees now. George went on chuckling. Down down came the parachute.

Emma was sitting now. Still chuckling,

*The parachute floated on down down down
and quietly covered them all.*

George put out his hand. Something dropped in her lap. *"Monster!"*

Monster grinned and grew until he was just the right size to sit comfortably next to her while the parachute floated on down down down and quietly covered them all.

"I didn't want it all white," Emma said.

A FRESH COAT OF PAINT

Emma stood in the doorway of her nearly empty bedroom. She looked at the ceiling, then at the walls, then at Dad perched on a ladder. He had a big paintbrush in his hand.

"I didn't want it all white," she said.

Dad left off painting for a moment. "I've got these two big tins of white paint that need using up, Emma. It looks very fresh and clean, don't you think?"

Emma had another quick look at the very white ceiling and the not so white walls. She shook her head. Her chin wobbled a bit.

Dad came down the ladder. Putting the tin of paint on the floor and the brush on top, he squatted beside her.

"Think how all the other colours will show up when we put your room straight. Bright books in your bookcase. Teddy's red suit. Your blue duvet. Why, you could hang a new picture on the wall just there. So you could lie in bed and look at it. How about that?"

Emma said in a wobbly voice, "I wanted *green* there and there," pointing at the window wall and the place where her

wardrobe usually stood. "And *yellow* there!" – pointing at the door wall. "And red behind my bed and a purple ceiling."

Dad raised his eyebrows. "You'd need sunglasses."

"No I wouldn't. Monster likes bright colours too."

"I think Monster should be satisfied with his new front door," Dad said.

Emma looked at the place where the

hole-under-her-bed used to be. Dad had made a new front door with proper hinges and a little doorknob, though it wasn't painted yet.

"Tell you what," he went on. "Let's see what other tins of paint we have downstairs. There might be a nice bright colour for the woodwork and for Monster's door. A compromise."

"What's com-prom-eyes?" Emma asked.

"You give in a bit and I give in a bit. So we agree in the end – like we did about that hole in the wall."

Emma understood. Dad had wanted to fill in the hole, until she told him Monster wouldn't be able to get out. Now there was a door which did both things.

They went downstairs, found two old tins of paint and took them back to Emma's bedroom.

*They found two old tins of paint
and took them back to Emma's bedroom*

Dad opened them up. "Brown and green. Not very bright and not enough of either to do all the woodwork."

"*I* know." Emma cheered up. "I've got a good idea. Why don't we mix them together, like at playschool. At playschool we have big saucers and we mix and mix and mix..."

"And end up with mud! I don't think Monster would like a muddy front door." Dad grinned and stood up. "I think the best plan is for me to nip to the shop and buy more paint. What colour do you like best?"

"Red," Emma said firmly.

"Red it is then!" Dad wiped his painty hands on a rag. "Shan't be a tick. George's dad is in the garden if you need anything." And he went out to the car.

Emma heard the car door slam. She went to the window. If she looked one way she could see Freda nibbling grass. If she looked the other way there was George's dad digging his vegetable plot. He waved at her. A bluebottle zoomed past like a tiny helicopter. Inside nobody was doing anything. It was very quiet. Until...

C-r-r-r-e-e-e-e-a-k...

Emma spun round. The new little door in the wall was inching open. From behind came one pointed ear. Then some wisps of wild wild hair. Next, a round red eye stared about. A flat nose sniffed the air. Another eye appeared. Another ear.

"It's all right," Emma said. "You can come out."

Monster sidled into the nearly empty bedroom. He gazed at the ladder, at the newspaper covering the floor. Then he spotted the tins of paint near the wall. Very slowly he began to walk his fingers across the newspaper, arm stretching like elastic. Up the side of the first tin walked his fingers, and ... off with the lid!

"I don't think..." Emma began, watching him flip the second lid on to the floor.

"I don't think we ought..." she went on, as he stirred first the green paint, then the brown, with a skinny finger.

"Dad won't..." Her eyes opened wide as Monster's elastic arm snapped small again, pulling the rest of him close to the tins.

"You might..." – she held her breath as he hopped on top of the tin of brown paint – "...FALL IN!" Breath and words burst out together just as Monster went *splat* right in the middle, sending up a shower of brown spots and a gurgly squeak.

Emma rushed to the tin and began to fish about, trying to help him. But Monster wouldn't keep still. His arms thrashed. His

Monster went splat *in the paint tin,
sending up a shower of brown spots.*

head shook. He wriggled his shoulders, sneezed paint from his nose, blew paint from his mouth. At last she managed to grip him round the middle, but just at that moment he decided to grow. His big hands grabbed at the top of the brown paint tin and landed in the green paint tin. Body swelling, all of him slippery, he shot from Emma's hand and hit the wall, arms outstretched. His green painty hands dabbed and grabbed as he tried to save himself. Scrawping, scratching, slithering, slipping, he landed with a wet *schlupp* on the floor.

Emma looked at the wall.

Brown streaks where Monster's stomach had slid. Brown and green patches where his hands had grabbed. Spots of brown dappling between. A scattering of green grass-stalk fingermarks at the bottom.

Emma looked at Monster.

He was scraping green fingers through his sticky brown hair. Rubbing brown goo from his gummy eyes. Slopping and skating as he got to his greasy feet. A chocolate Monster!

"Come here!" she said.

Monster squelched across the newspaper and stood beside her.

"Look!" she pointed to the wall. "You've made a tree. It's a summer tree because it's summer now. But it needs more leaves."

They both looked at Dad's paintbrush. Then at each other. Emma shook her head. Monster did the same, spraying her with brown and green from his wild painty hair. Spraying the floor as well, and a bit of the wall.

"*I* know," Emma said. "I've got a good idea. Why don't *you* be my paintbrush? Your hair is just right. Only you must shrink a bit so I can hold you."

Emma wrapped Monster's middle in a strip of newspaper, and dipped his hair into the green tin.

Monster gave a sneeze of surprise, but obligingly shrank. Emma wrapped his middle in a strip of newspaper so he wouldn't slip out of her hand. Dipping his hair into the green tin, she began to paint more leaves on the tree. She painted some round the edge, some in the middle and a few at the bottom: "Because the wind blew them off."

She added more grass stalks and a green bird on a brown branch, and a spade leaning against the trunk: "So George's dad can dig if he wants."

Then she stood back to see what was left to paint.

"EMMA!" roared Dad's voice. "WHAT DO YOU THINK YOU ARE DOING? JUST LOOK AT YOURSELF!"

Emma jumped. She had been so busy she hadn't heard the car come back, or Dad's feet on the stairs. She looked down at her front. Brown smears on her T-shirt, green on her knees, more green on her socks and shoes. Her hands were splodged with green and brown. She still held the strip of newspaper, but her Monster paintbrush had vanished.

"He's gone!" she looked round and saw paint marks on Monster's tiny doorknob.

"Who's gone?"

"Monster. He was being my brush ... I was finishing the last little bit." Her voice got smaller and smaller because Dad looked so cross.

"Little bit? *Little bit!*" Dad's voice got louder and louder. "YOU CALL THAT A LITTLE BIT? I CALL THAT A BIG MESS ALL OVER MY NEW PAINT AND I DON'T WANT ANY MORE OF THAT MONSTER NONSENSE!"

Emma was getting cross now. "It's not a

"Little bit? Little bit!"
Dad's voice got louder and louder.

mess. It's a tree. And Monster isn't nonsense. He painted most. He fell in the paint tin, then fell against the wall. Then I borrowed him to use as my paintbrush. We did the tree together. And don't shout! *You* said I could have a picture on my wall just there. You *said* – where I can see it when I'm in bed. *You said* ... remember?"

Very carefully Dad bent down and put the new tin of red paint on the floor. When he straightened up again the corners of his mouth were twitching.

Emma saw the smile grow. "Can I keep the picture?" She held his painty hand.

"Well," Dad said at last. "The walls need a second coat, but I daresay I could paint round your tree."

"Com-prom-eyes!" Emma looked down at herself again. "I need a wash."

"A sponge down with turps, then a bath,

more like," Dad said. "Come on. It's nearly time for tea."

"Monster needs lots of turps," Emma told him as they went downstairs. "And bubbles in his bath. Can I have bubbles too?"

"Stop being silly," Emma told Monster.
"We've got things to do."

MONSTER SNOWMAN

Monster was dotting about the winter garden. He jumped in and out of snowdrifts, shouting and hurling handfuls of the snow high in the air. He was in a dotty mood.

"Stop being silly," Emma said. "We've got things to do. It's Dad's birthday today. We're going to make a snowman for his present."

She had thought of this as soon as she had woken up that morning and seen the shining snow outside. Straight after breakfast she had put on her boots and anorak, found her bobble cap, dragged her old seaside bucket and spade from the cupboard under the stairs.

Now she was in the garden.

"Come on!" She started to walk across the snowgrass.

Monster took no notice. "WHEEEESH!" He sprang about, puffing his chest, then rolling in the snow until he looked like a furry white pin-cushion.

"Aren't you going to help?" Emma pointed at the bucket. "You can have that if you like. Fill it with snow and empty it here." She chose a place under the apple tree. "He's got to be a big snowman. As big as me." She began to dig, piling up snow and patting it firm with her spade.

Monster didn't pick up the bucket. He gave her a sideways look.

"BLOOOOSH!" he yelled, bouncing at her all of a sudden.

Emma almost fell over. "STOP IT!" She jabbed at him with her spade. "That's not helping!"

He darted out of reach behind the apple tree – grinning at her.

Emma went back to her digging. Slowly the snowman began to grow. He had almost reached her middle when something cold and wet was pushed down the back of her neck, under her jersey.

"URGH!" She jumped round in time to see Monster's very long thin arm snap back behind the tree trunk. His head poked out. Thumbs in his ears, he waggled his skinny fingers, making teasing shivery noises: "CHUCHUCHUCHUCH!"

"Why don't you say real words?" Emma said crossly. She had her shoulders squeezed up and was trying to fish out the ice-cold snow. She couldn't quite reach. "Just you wait!" Scooping some snow, she flung it at him.

Monster dodged. Peeked out from the

The air was soon full of whizzing snowballs.

other side of the tree. Ducked ... but not quick enough.

Smack! Snow in his ear.

Emma laughed.

Monster dug out the snow with a long skinny finger, shaking his head. Making grumbling noises under his breath.

"Say *real* words!" Emma threw another snowball, hitting his nose.

"FROO ... FROOSHIPAH ... AAAAAAH ... *atishooo!*" Monster sneezed, blowing out snowbits. His furry feet stamped, kicking up a small snowstorm.

Emma kicked with her boots.

Scuffling, scooping, rolling, hurling ... the air was soon full of whizzing snowballs, snowchips, grass scraps, bits of earth, flaky dead leaves. They tumbled over. Scrambled up giggling. Tripped again, because the bucket was in the way, then the spade, then their own feet. Snow patched their elbows, their knees, stuck in their hair, stuffed noses and ears.

At last they had to stop for breath.

Emma looked at the messy garden. The snowgrass was grey and scuffed. Monster-tracks ringed the apple tree. Emma-tracks walked across Dad's vegetable plot. The poor snowman was spotted with dirt. She grabbed her spade.

"He needs more snow," she told Monster. "Lots more. Lots and lots or he won't be ready by dinner time."

But Monster didn't seem bothered. It had begun to snow again and he capered away, head back, mouth open, licking up snowflakes with his long yellow tongue. Not seeing the thin skim of ice on the path.

His feet suddenly skidded. Arms waving,

Emma looked at the messy garden.

*A crack opened where Emma had meant
to put the snowman's buttons.*

he came skating wildly towards Emma. Past her … and plunged head first into the bottom of the snowman.

Emma dropped her spade. "Are you all right?"

The top of the snowman shook. Bits of his sides fell down. A crack opened where Emma had meant to put his buttons. More of him started to slither and slip.

Monster sat up. "OOOFP!" He rubbed the top of his head.

"EMMA!" Dad bellowed from the kitchen. "COME AND GET READY. WE'RE GOING FOR FISH AND CHIPS. I'M NOT COOKING TODAY."

Emma stared at the sad tumbledown snowman. At his rumpled dirty coat. At the crack in his front where the buttons should be. Together, she and Monster stared at the hole Monster's head had made.

"HURRY UP, EMMA!" Dad shouted.

Emma blinked. Her chin wobbled.

Monster got up. He patted her arm. "URRRRG!" he growled softly. "PRRRUFFL!" He began to roll in the snow.

Emma went back to the house, scuffling her feet. "I haven't finished your present," she told Dad indoors.

"Never mind," Dad said. He helped her change into dry clothes.

"I'll finish after the fish and chips." Emma cheered up. She liked fish and chips.

But after fish and chips they went to see a film in a cinema. And after that, George's mum had made a special birthday tea – ice-cream and a cake with twenty-five candles. Emma helped Dad blow them out. It was dark by home time.

As they walked across George's garden to the gate in the fence, Emma remembered the snowman.

"I didn't finish your present!" Her voice wobbled a bit.

"Finish it tomorrow," Dad suggested.

"It won't be a *birthday* present tomorrow."

"Yes it will, if you tell me what it is today," Dad said.

"A snowman," Emma told him as they went through the gate. "But I wanted to finish him *today*!"

"He looks finished to me," Dad said.

The moon was round and very bright in the sky. It shone on the snowgrass, the apple tree, and on something else. Something huge and white, like a big snowball. Emma could hardly believe her eyes. She went up close. It wasn't *her* snowman. This snowman had feet at the bottom and arms that stuck out at the sides. She knocked on the front. "Monster?"

Dad walked all the way round. "A

splendid monster snowman. Let's finish him together shall we? All he needs is a couple of eyes and a nose."

While he fetched coal for the eyes and a carrot for the nose, Emma found three pebbles to make buttons.

"My very best present." Dad gave her a hug. He took off his cap and put it on top of the snowman's head.

Emma smiled and yawned. Making a snowman was very hard work.

"Bedtime," Dad said.

★ ★ ★

Emma lay in bed. The moon came in and made silver stripes on her wall. A moth flew round and round and round. She was almost asleep when...

"MMMMM!"

What was that noise? But her eyelids were too tired to open.

"My very best present."
Dad gave Emma a hug.

Then something cold and wet patted her cheek.

"MMMMMUH!"

A tug at her hair.

This time she managed to open her eyes. Monster was there. Melting snow dripped from his wild wet hair, from his flat purple nose and pointed ears, making a puddle round his damp feet.

Emma stared. "*What* did you say?"

He gave her a shivery grin. "EHMMUH!" he growled, and held out Dad's cap.

★ ★ ★

"Our splendid snowman has gone," Dad said to Emma at breakfast next morning. "Nearly all the snow melted last night."

Emma nodded. "I know. Monster told me. He wanted to come down and tell *you* ... to show how he can say real words now. But I made him stay in bed because he's got a bad cold today. So he asked me to give you this –" and she put Dad's cap on the table.

THE

END